**BUDDABUGS**

Mindful Fun, for Little Ones

# ZENJI
# & the Muzzy Bug

Written & Illustrated by
## Aisli Madden

THE
MINDFUL
& MAGICAL
SLEEP
SOLUTION!

Zenji the Buddabug was feeling very WOOZY.

His chest was wheezy, his forehead was clammy and his whole body ached.

In fact he was feeling rather Cranky indeed!

Zenji had caught a Muzzy Bug!

Zenji was bored.

The Muzzy Bug was contagious so he couldn't play with his friends. Instead he played with Teddy, who wasn't much fun at all.

"I'm so miserable," Zenji cried.

"Don't feel sad!" said a little voice out of thin air.

"Did you speak, Teddy?!" Zenji asked, as he peeped over his blanket in shock.

"It wasn't Teddy... it was me!"
the little voice said.

"My name is Karma.
I'm the little voice that
lives inside your head."

Zenji looked down and saw
a tiny Buddabug glowing
beside his bed. Karma looked
exactly like Zenji only
much, much smaller.

"Everybody has a
little magic inside them,"
Karma whispered.

"You just need to
believe in yourself."

"If you FOCUS on this moment, you can make magical things happen."

With that, Karma floated slowly above Zenji's bed and began to chant...

"Lie on your back
with your eyelids closed,

Now clench all your fingers
and wrinkle your nose,

Stretch your legs out
as long as they go,

Then relax
your whole body
from your head
to your toes..."

"Breathe in
happy thoughts that
make you feel glad,
Then exhale
all the yucky ones
that make you
feel sad.

Scary things boogeymen
meanies
Yuckiness Cuts & nightmares
Bruises
Bullies Ghosts
Monsters
Worry Teasing
Muzzy Bugs

# Do this three times

and soon you will see, that there's **oodles** of **magic,** in the **air** that you **breathe."**

Friends
Playing
Cuddles
Family
Teddy Bears
Buddabugzz
Love
Magic
Giggles
Kisses
Smiles
FUN
Happiness

As Zenji listened to Karma
he **focused**
on each breath he took,

and each breath he took
made him sleepier and
**sleepier.**

Then slowly but surely,
**Zenji began to
shrink!**

The sleepier Zenji grew,
the **smaller**
and smaller
and smaller,
he shrank...

until he became so small...

...he floated inside his own body!

Zenji drifted

down,

down,

down,

deep into his chest, where he found tell-tale signs of the

Muzzy Bug.

"If I **focus** on this moment, I can make **magical things** happen," Zenji thought.

Suddenly, **sparkling white light** gushed from his fingertips!

He pointed this **light** at the Muzzy Bug and...

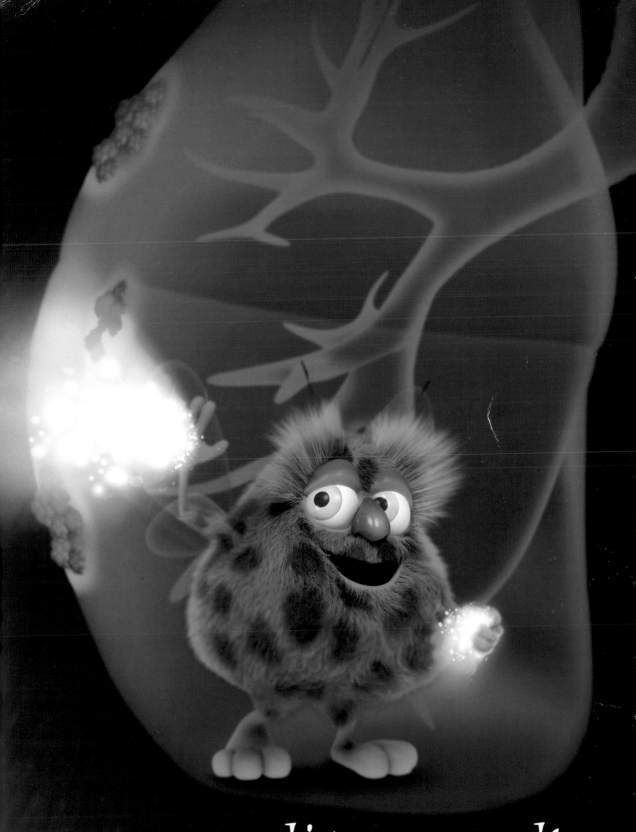

...the Muzzy Bug disappeared!

And Zenji became
# even more
# sleepy!

Once again,
the sleepier Zenji grew,
the **smaller**
and smaller
and smaller,
he shrank,
until he became
so small...

...that he whizzed through
his body, like a super cool
water-park slide...

...shining
**magical light**
everywhere he went!

He travelled from
the tips of his toes,
up through his legs,
to his tummy
and then into his arms...

...pointing light at
the places where the
Muzzy Bug had been.

He pointed light at his
heart
and it glittered
and glistened
and glowed with
love!

With every breath Zenji took,
the light became brighter
and brighter
and brighter,
until it was so bright
his whole body
twinkled and sparkled with
magical light.

Zenji felt strong
and healthy
and happier than he had
ever been before...

...But he was still very,
very sleepy!

"Good night Zenji,"
Karma whispered.

And with that, Zenji drifted
into a deep, deep sleep,
where the darkness of night
was lit by his light
and he forgot
that he had ever caught
a Muzzy Bug!

The End.

Zenji likes
to dream that he
is flying through
fluffy clouds
with his friends...